Michael and Jane Pelusey

THE MEDIA
Photography

CHELSEA HOUSE
PUBLISHERS
A Haights Cross Communications Company ®
Philadelphia

This edition first published in 2006 in the United States of America by Chelsea House Publishers, a subsidiary of Haights Cross Communications.

A Haights Cross Communications Company ®

Chelsea House Publishers
2080 Cabot Boulevard West, Suite 201
Langhorne, PA 19047-1813

The Chelsea House world wide web address is www.chelseahouse.com

First published in 2005 by
MACMILLAN EDUCATION AUSTRALIA PTY LTD
627 Chapel Street, South Yarra 3141

Visit our website at www.macmillan.com.au

Associated companies and representatives throughout the world.

Library of Congress Cataloging-in-Publication Data applied for.
ISBN 0 7910 8805 7

Edited by Anne Löhnberg and Angelique Campbell-Muir
Text and cover design by Ivan Finnegan, iF Design
All photographs and images used in design © Pelusey Photography.
Cover photograph: Sports photographer, courtesy of Pelusey Photography.

Printed in China

Acknowledgments
Michael and Jane Pelusey would like to thank Paul Young of Nautilus Photographics, Rod McLeod of Lumiere Photographics, Churchill Color Laboratories and Scarborough Photographics for their assistance.
The publisher is grateful to the following for permission to reproduce copyright material:

All photographs courtesy of Pelusey Photography.

While every care has been taken to trace and acknowledge copyright, the publisher tenders their apologies for any accidental infringement where copyright has proved untraceable. Where the attempt has been unsuccessful, the publisher welcomes information that would redress the situation.

CONTENTS

When a word is printed in bold, you can look up its meaning in the glossary on page 31.

THE MEDIA

People communicate in many different ways. One thing common to all forms of communication is that a message is conveyed. Communicating is about spreading information and sharing it with others, in spoken and written words as well as in pictures.

The different means we use to communicate are called media. Each of them is designed to spread information and news, entertain people, or let them share experiences. The audience can be one person or a million. Forms of communication that reach millions of people at the same time are called mass media. They include:

◎ photography
◎ film and television
◎ the Internet
◎ magazines
◎ newspapers
◎ radio.

The media have great influence in our everyday lives. They inform us about current events, expose us to advertising, and entertain us.

Media play an important role in a family's life.

PHOTOGRAPHY

A photograph (or photo) captures a moment in time as an image.

Showing us the world

Through photography, we can see many things around the world. Photographs allow us to see beautiful places and show us how people in different countries live their lives in different ways. They convey a message, using pictures instead of words. Some photographers have become famous for capturing images that change our lives.

News and entertainment

Photography plays a vital part in other media, such as newspapers, magazines, and the Internet. Browse through the magazines at any newsstand and you will see photographs showing images of nature, sports, or outer space; portraits and snapshots of famous people; and pictures of historic events. The advertising industry often uses photographs to grab our attention and sell a product.

Photography as art

Many photographs are beautiful to look at or bring out powerful emotions in the viewer. They are often considered works of art, just like paintings. Collections of photographs are regularly shown as exhibitions in art galleries.

Examples of art photography

EARLY PHOTOGRAPHY

A Frenchman called Joseph Nicéphore Niépce took the first photograph in 1826. He joined Louis Jacques Daguerre to experiment further. The early cameras were large wooden boxes. They were very slow, taking up to eight hours to take a photograph. Research helped make cameras smaller and much faster.

By the 1850s, photography was a real industry. At first, photographers mainly took pictures of people posing for the camera. Then photographers began to travel the world, as cameras became smaller and easier to operate. They brought back images that thrilled people and sometimes frightened them. The first war photographs were taken during the **Crimean War** in the 1850s. They made the horrors of war very clear.

Around 1900, cameras were easy to operate, but still quite large and cumbersome. In the 1920s, the Leica company produced a compact camera that used **35-millimeter film**. This camera allowed photographers the freedom to go anywhere, not hampered by heavy equipment.

A family portrait, taken in the early 1900s

Media photographers

Famous magazines, such as *National Geographic* and *LIFE*, were quick to take advantage of the new freedom in photography. They sent photographers to cover events throughout the world. Media photographers at war zones, sporting events, and festivals show the rest of the world what is happening.

Many magazines depend on eye-catching photos to help them sell.

Digital cameras

Today, photography is undergoing huge changes, caused by advances in **digital** photography and computer technology. Digital cameras do not use film; instead, they produce images that can be read by a computer.

A photographer can use a laptop computer to e-mail images to a newspaper or magazine office immediately after taking them. In most Western countries, digital cameras are now selling better than cameras that use film.

NEWS FLASH

COPYRIGHT

Photographs are usually owned by the photographer who takes them. In legal terms, he or she has the copyright. This also applies to digital photos on the Internet. Many Websites state who owns the images and that they cannot be used by other people without permission. The symbol for copyright is ©.

TYPES OF PHOTOGRAPHY

Photography as a medium has many different specialties. Each specialty has a different role in communicating visual messages to people.

Photojournalism

In photojournalism, the story of an event is told through pictures. Usually, the photojournalist takes a series of photographs. These photographs are placed in a magazine in a certain order, so the reader can follow the story without needing many words. *LIFE* magazine became famous during the 1960s for using this style of **documentary** photography.

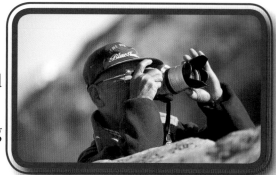

A photojournalist working on location

A feature article in a magazine

GOLD FEVER

Press photography

Newspapers hire press photographers to take photographs of events that are of interest to their readers. The photographer tries to capture the most important aspect of the event, because usually only one photograph will be published with a news article.

Feature-article photography

Often, photos are used to illustrate feature articles in a newspaper or magazine. Feature articles are longer and more detailed than general news stories. They can cover general-interest subjects such as fashion, food, and travel. Often, more than one photo is used to help tell the story or to draw in the reader.

Advertising photography

Most advertisements include a photograph to get their message across. An advertising agency comes up with a theme to sell a product. The product is then photographed in a way that makes the public want to buy it.

Billboards advertising fruit and vegetables in a train station

Commercial photography

Businesses use photography to promote themselves. A car company may need photographs of the latest car model to use in its company brochures, annual report, and sales catalogs.

Celebrity photography

The public likes to see photographs of movie stars, pop stars, and other famous people going about their daily lives. **Paparazzi** photographers may follow celebrities to a restaurant, take photos of them, and then sell the photographs to magazines and newspapers.

Social and family photography

People who are enjoying themselves socially often take photographs. Sometimes they employ a photographer to record important events for future generations.

A wedding photographer at work in South Korea

Art photography

By using different angles and creative lighting to create a certain effect, a photographer can produce visual works of art. Many art galleries display photographs as well as paintings and other artworks.

WORKING IN PHOTOGRAPHY

Many skills and processes are involved in creating a photograph. Sometimes one person does all the jobs. In other cases, a team of people works together to produce the final product.

The photographer

Photographers take photographs. They must have a talent for seeing the best angles and **composition**. They have several cameras to use on any occasion. A photographer may do one type of photography or many, indoors and outdoors. Some photographers **develop** their own film.

A photographer takes a photograph in his studio.

The photographic assistant

A photographer may need help carrying heavy cameras, light stands, and other equipment. Assistants often hope to become photographers themselves. They take on the job of being an assistant to gain experience.

The laboratory technician

Once the photographs have been taken, digitally or on film, the next step is to produce a photograph that people can see. Films need to be developed. Technicians in a photographic laboratory use special equipment, chemicals, and techniques to process the film. Depending on the type of film, they then produce a set of prints or **transparencies**. Technicians can print photographs in any size, from film or digital files.

A laboratory technician develops transparencies.

Photo library staff

If a company or magazine needs a specific photograph, sometimes it can be found at a photo library. A photo library has many thousands of images on file for customers to choose from. The photo library staff search through the many photos to find one that matches the customer's request. The company pays the library for the right to use the photograph. The photographer who took the photograph receives a payment from the library every time his or her photo is used.

Models

Fashion photographers usually use models when they photograph clothing, jewelry, and hairstyles. Model agencies hire out models of all body shapes and skin tones. There are even agencies that supply animal models such as dogs, cats, and horses.

Fashion models in magazines

The graphic designer

Graphic designers arrange words, artwork, and photographs together in a way that will have the right impact on the viewer. When you see a dramatic poster or an eye-catching brochure, it has usually been put together by a graphic designer.

A graphic designer at his computer

11

FROM IDEA TO PHOTOGRAPH

Every photograph begins with an idea. This is the first stage in creating a photographic image. After the idea, there are several other important stages to go through before the photograph is finished. The stages on the flow chart below show how a photograph is created. Photographers working in different fields go through these steps when they take photos for a particular job.

Stage 1 — IDEAS

Ideas for photographs come from many sources. They can come from the photographer's own mind or from a company or organization that hires the photographer.

Stage 2 — PLANNING

The photographer researches how the photograph is to be used in the publication. This influences how he or she approaches the subject.

Stage 3 — PREPARATION AND EQUIPMENT

Sometimes special equipment may be needed for the photograph. The photographer chooses the right cameras, film, and other equipment for each particular assignment.

Photography case studies

Read the six stages from idea to photograph on pages 14–23 for three different photography case studies:

CASE STUDY 1
A kayak trip promotion

CASE STUDY 2
A newspaper article

CASE STUDY 3
A photographic book

Finding the right angle

Read the six stages from idea to photograph on pages 14–23

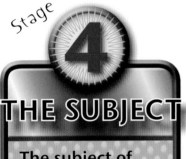

Stage

4
THE SUBJECT

The subject of the photograph should be its main focus. The photographer achieves this by putting the subject in a well-chosen position in the photo and by the choice of background, foreground, and lighting.

Stage

5
LIGHTING AND COMPOSITION

Lighting and composition are the most important factors that determine the impact an image has on the viewer.

Stage

6
PHOTOGRAPHIC PROCESSING

The exposed film is removed from the camera and processed. In the case of a digital camera, the image is downloaded onto a computer. The final image is then ready to use.

Coming up with ideas for photographs is a creative process. A photograph should visually tell a story to sell a product, match a newspaper article, or illustrate a book.

Stage
1

CASE STUDY 1

A KAYAK TRIP PROMOTION

The owner of a tour company offering kayaking trips wants to promote his business. He is thinking of advertisements, articles in magazines, and a slide show. He contacts Thea, a photographer, to take pictures of his kayaking trips.

The tour operator wants to sell kayaking trips to people of all ages.

Stage
1

CASE STUDY 2

A NEWSPAPER ARTICLE

Community members are setting up a conservation group to look after a local nature area. The local newspaper is going to publish an article about them. The editor of the newspaper wants a photograph to illustrate the article. She gives the newspaper photographer, Lindsay, details about the group.

Stage
1

CASE STUDY 3

A PHOTOGRAPHIC BOOK

David is a photographer who travels around the world, taking photographs of people going about their everyday lives in village markets. He is planning to publish a beautiful book of his photographs.

David taking photographs on the streets of Honduras

The photographer plans what is going to be in the photograph. He or she asks:
◎   How many photographs will tell the story, and how will they be used?
◎   How will the image capture people's attention?

Stage 2

CASE STUDY 1

A KAYAK TRIP PROMOTION
Thea will go on the kayaking trips and take a range of photographs. Because the aim is to attract people to kayaking, she hopes for blue skies and clear water. If the weather is bad, the assignment will be postponed.

Thea plans to photograph all aspects of the trip, including the preparations beforehand.

Stage 2

CASE STUDY 2

A NEWSPAPER ARTICLE
There will only be one photograph with the article, which should show the people involved in the campaign and the area they want to protect. Lindsay contacts a member of the environmental group and arranges to meet them in the area.

The photo will show the people and the nature area they want to save.

Stage 2

CASE STUDY 3

A PHOTOGRAPHIC BOOK
David's book will include many photographs. It will be divided into chapters: people, transportation, and produce. David has researched where in the world colorful markets are held and on which days. He has planned his travels around these market days.

3 PREPARATION AND EQUIPMENT

Each style of photography requires different photographic equipment. The photographer decides what will be the best camera and lenses to use. For sporting events where the photographer cannot stand close to the action, a **telephoto lens** may be needed.

Many busy newspaper photographers prefer to use digital cameras. This way, no time is wasted developing and processing film. For **glossy** magazines and books, many photographers still use transparencies, because they give a better-quality image.

Different cameras, a compact tripod, and rolls of slide film on a waterproof bag. The camera on the left is waterproof.

Stage 3 CASE STUDY 1

A KAYAK TRIP PROMOTION

Thea needs to be well-prepared, because she will be spending several days taking photos in locations a long way from home. She cannot go back if she runs out of film or a camera breaks. Thea brings more than enough transparency film and several cameras, just in case. She also brings a **tripod**.

The cameras could easily get wet on this assignment. Thea uses waterproof bags to keep them dry. Thea also has an underwater camera to use in situations when the camera will get wet.

Lindsay checks his equipment before the photo shoot.

Stage

3

CASE STUDY 2

A NEWSPAPER ARTICLE

Lindsay uses a digital camera, because that makes it easy to send the images to the newspaper. He checks that the camera is working. To be on the safe side, he brings a spare camera and batteries. A flat battery or faulty camera could ruin a **photo shoot**. Lindsay is very busy, since he has to take photographs of six different subjects today.

Stage

3

CASE STUDY 3

A PHOTOGRAPHIC BOOK

David has thousands of transparencies from his travels to choose from. It is not an easy task to select the photographs for his book. David has to pick out 200 of the best images to go in the book. This is called editing. David uses a **light desk** to view and sort the transparencies. He uses a special magnifying glass to detect any images that are not perfect.

Going through the market slides on the light desk

4 THE SUBJECT

The subject is what a photograph is about. The challenge for the photographer is to capture the subject at the point of greatest impact. The famous French photographer Henri Cartier-Bresson called this the "decisive moment." It could be the fleeting smile of a village girl or a child jumping across a puddle.

The angle the photographer chooses is also important. Seen from down low, the subject will appear big and powerful. Looking down from a high angle can make the subject look small and meek.

Stage

4

CASE STUDY 1

A KAYAK TRIP PROMOTION

The subject of Thea's photographs is the people who are enjoying kayaking in a beautiful location. Thea takes many different photographs to capture the whole experience. She photographs the participants getting safety lessons before they set out in the kayaks. She also shoots nature scenes. Most importantly, Thea photographs people paddling in kayaks.

Thea takes a range of photos to capture all aspects of kayaking.

Lindsay takes a photo
of the environmental
activist group.

CASE STUDY 2

A NEWSPAPER ARTICLE

The subjects of Lindsay's photograph are the group
of activists and the nature area they wish to save. He
looks for the best possible angle, composition, and light
to create a memorable photograph that will capture
readers' attention. Lindsay asks the women to crouch and
look at the weeds that need to be cleared from the area.
He gets down low to take the photographs, so the weeds
will be clearly visible.

CASE STUDY 3

A PHOTOGRAPHIC BOOK

Every photograph chosen for David's book must
relate to the main theme of the book. David chooses
images that will draw in the readers and make them
feel like they are at the market themselves. This book
is really a form of photojournalism, because the
collection tells a story of life in a village market.

David's photos capture
the atmosphere of the
village markets.

Stage 5 LIGHTING AND COMPOSITION

A photographer always looks for the best possible light to photograph the subject. Natural sunlight changes, depending on the time of day and how cloudy it is. Most landscape photographers prefer the light in the early morning or late afternoon. This is because the sun's rays are coming in at a low angle, producing more intense colors. If there is not enough natural light, the photographer can use an electronic flash or **studio lighting**.

Composition is the art of placing objects in a photograph in a way that is pleasing to the eye. Most photographers avoid placing the main subject in the middle of the photograph.

CASE STUDY 1

A KAYAK TRIP PROMOTION

The kayaking trips take place during daylight hours, and when the weather is good. There are plenty of rest stops on the trips, so Thea uses those times to take beautiful sunny photographs. She shoots some of the images in the late afternoon, to make use of the better light. She also takes photographs on the beach at dusk, after the day's adventures. As Thea is taking many pictures, she can experiment with the light and composition.

A kayak on the beach at sunset

Lindsay and the activists look at the images on the back of the digital camera.

CASE STUDY 2

A NEWSPAPER ARTICLE

Lindsay's picture of the environmental group is taken in the afternoon. He uses a flash on the camera to make the shadows on the people's faces lighter. After taking several photographs from different angles, Lindsay reviews the images, to make sure he has some photos he is satisfied with. He can do this right away, looking at the digital display on the camera.

CASE STUDY 3

A PHOTOGRAPHIC BOOK

David likes to take photographs during the early morning or late afternoon, when the light is at its most interesting. David chooses images that vary in their composition to keep the photographs in his book interesting for the reader. He has close-up shots of food for sale, portraits of people, and views of patterns or textures, such as the colorful patterns on people's clothes.

The repetition of colors and shapes makes this photo of a vibrant market in Guatemala a good image.

6 PHOTOGRAPHIC PROCESSING

After the photographs have been taken, the images need to be converted to a form that people can see and work with. For photographic film, the first step is processing the film. Special equipment with chemicals is used to develop the film and print the photographs. Digital pictures are downloaded onto a computer. Special programs can be used to make changes to the images. They can then be sent to a designer or printer.

Stage

6

CASE STUDY 1

A KAYAK TRIP PROMOTION

Thea has taken many rolls of transparency film on the kayaking trips. After returning home, she takes the films to a professional laboratory to be processed and framed. She then labels her transparencies and takes them to the tour operator. Thea and the tour operator go through the transparencies together. They select images for different purposes. Some of the photographs are sent to a graphic designer, who uses them in a brochure.

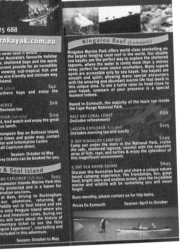

The final kayaking brochure

Lindsay makes adjustments to his digital photograph on the computer.

CASE STUDY 2

A NEWSPAPER ARTICLE

Lindsay returns to the newspaper office and downloads the photographs onto his computer. After the best picture is chosen, Lindsay uses a photo manipulation program to make some parts of the image lighter. This way, it will look good when it is printed in the newspaper in black and white. The photograph is then placed on the newspaper page along with the article.

CASE STUDY 3

A PHOTOGRAPHIC BOOK

Once David has chosen the 200 photographs for his book, he sends them to the publisher, together with the text. Graphic designers lay out the photographs and words. The designed pages are sent back to David for his approval. After the final go-ahead, the material is sent to a printer for printing. It may take 12 months or more before David's book reaches bookstore shelves.

The market photographs are scanned so they can be laid out on a computer.

Market People

Lake Inle market, Myanmar

Chichicastenango market, Guatemala

DELIVERING THE MESSAGE

We live in a very visual world. During our daily lives, we constantly see photographs in one form or another.

Advertisements

Millions of photographs are used in advertising, to convince people to buy a product or use a service. We see advertising in magazines and newspapers, on public billboards, in shopping catalogs and company brochures. The photographs are taken in such a way that the subject seems to jump out at you, saying, "Buy me!" It is no coincidence that during the cold winter months, travel companies advertise tours to tropical islands using images of palm-fringed beaches, blue skies, and crystal-clear waters.

Travel brochures are full of attractive photographs.

Newspapers and magazines

Newspapers and magazines use photographs to support or illustrate their written articles. The picture editor of a newspaper or magazine spends many hours choosing the photographs that best suit the articles. One of the biggest jobs is selecting an image for the front cover. A striking photograph on the front cover means more copies will be sold at newsstands.

Front covers of magazines that capture the eye

Art galleries

Galleries are places for displaying art. They can feature paintings and sculptures, but also collections of photographs. The photographs are printed, framed, and hung on the walls for people to admire. These can be images that make a statement about our society, or that are simply beautiful to look at. Photos can be displayed on their own, or in groups, to tell a story.

Preparing for a photographic exhibition

A selection of coffee-table books

Books

Photographs can be presented in books, either with text or by themselves. These are often large hardcover books with glossy paper, presenting beautiful, colorful photographs at their very best. Such books are known as coffee-table books, because people like to have them lying around so visitors can browse through them.

Audiovisual presentations

Some photographers use projectors and screens to show their images in audiovisual presentations, such as slide shows. An audiovisual presentation is like a movie, but with still pictures. The presentations are designed to take the people in the audience on a journey, to entertain them, or educate them. They can be presented using slides or using digital images and special computer programs.

CAREERS IN PHOTOGRAPHY

Photography is a rich and rewarding area to work in for people who have some artistic flair.

Bill at work at a sporting event

Bill is a sports photographer

"I took a photography course at a college. After completing my degree, I became a professional photographer. With my own business I got work photographing sporting events and football teams. I go to every football game in my home city."

Rod looks at some of his work in his studio.

Rod is a commercial photographer

"I studied photography at college. We learned all styles and types of photography, but the creativity of commercial and advertising photography interested me the most. I now have my own studio."

Paul is a landscape photographer

"I starting taking photos as a hobby. Friends started buying my photographs, and then more people saw them. I now sell my framed photographs in galleries and tourist shops."

Paul frames one of his prints.

Luciana runs a photographic laboratory

Luciana processes a customer's photographs.

"Since I was a child I have had a passion for photography and it became a hobby. I went into processing photographs around 15 years ago. Today I still love taking photographs, and often take photographs for my friends and family. People who want their photos developed and printed come to me. We have just changed all the equipment, since many people now have digital cameras."

Dave is a laboratory technician

Dave prints a poster-sized photograph.

"In high school, I got a part-time job at a photographic laboratory. After school, that became a full-time job, because I enjoyed the work. I specialized in processing transparencies, and later got work at a professional laboratory. Professional photographers bring in transparencies to be made into beautiful glossy prints."

Greg manipulates digital images

Greg corrects the color of an image on the computer.

"After school, I began to work in a photographic laboratory, processing film. Then the digital technology came in. To move with the times, I learned how to work with digital images. I learned on the job. There were no formal digital courses back then."

PHOTOGRAPHY IN SOCIETY

Photographs in the media have an influence on our everyday lives. On any one day, we may see hundreds or even thousands of photographs.

Documentation of events

Photographs document events that are happening around the world. This allows us to understand how people live in other places. A striking image can bring awareness of other people's tragic circumstances. It is hard to forget photographs of children starving in a famine or victims of war.

The downside is that photographs can be manipulated to change the meaning of what actually happened. One famous newspaper photograph showed a tank bearing down on some frightened people during a war. The photographer took the photo at an angle, not showing that the tank was actually part of a war memorial display and that it could not move. This photograph was used to mislead people.

Manipulating an image has become much easier with today's digital technology. A digital photograph on a computer can be changed radically and passed off as an original image. Some publications state that they have used a manipulated image, but many do not. What is real?

The original image of a beach

The same image, manipulated on a computer

Advertising photographs are everywhere around us.

Advertising

People are visual beings, so photos are used in advertisements. The photos are used to try to persuade viewers that they would look great in a particular outfit or fancy car. Just look at any magazine and count the advertisements that include photographs. Some advertising photographs create unrealistic expectations. Models' faces are sometimes touched up digitally, to make them look perfect.

Entertainment

Photography entertains us. We learn about other people's lives. Images of pop stars and television and movie stars are in demand for magazines and newspapers. Paparazzi photographers follow stars day and night, trying to get a revealing image. Is this an invasion of their privacy or just part of being famous?

Beautiful photos of spectacular scenery, animals, or people enjoying themselves make us feel good about the world. Glossy travel magazines, calendars, coffee-table books, and cookbooks use these kinds of photographs.

Celebrity magazines

A historical record

Photographs record visually how people live at a certain moment. Old photos show us how people in the past lived and worked, and what they wore. Photographs, along with words, tell us about important events that have shaped our lives. They have shown us the horrors of war and the first man on the moon.

THE FUTURE OF PHOTOGRAPHY

The demand for high-quality photography grows as humans explore new technical possibilities.

Advanced cameras are placed on satellites to take photographs of stars and other objects in space. They take much clearer photos than is possible from Earth, because there are no clouds or hazy atmosphere in space. In 2002, astronauts from a space shuttle replaced a camera on the **Hubble telescope**, which orbits around the Earth in space. It sends us images of distant galaxies that have never been seen or photographed before.

An astronomer adjusts the camera of a telescope on Earth.

The digital age

As technology advances, it is likely that digital photographs will completely replace film. Scientists are trying to create digital cameras with a better image quality than that of today's film cameras. When this happens, photographic film may become a thing of the past.

Digital cameras make it easier to take and process photographs, but that does not mean they always produce great images. Creative photography skills are still needed for that to happen—and those come from humans, not machines.

Pictures like this one of the Horse Head Nebula are taken by cameras on space satellites.

GLOSSARY

35-millimeter film commonly used type of film strip in photo cameras, with a width of 35 millimeters

composition the way parts of the picture are placed within the frame of the photograph

Crimean War a war from 1854 to 1856, in which Britain and France fought Russia over the rights to religious sites in Jerusalem and Nazareth

develop to apply a chemical process to a strip of film, so that it can be used to produce photographic prints

digital computer-based; using an electronic signal that carries information using numbers

documentary a factual representation of an event or a person's life

glossy shiny

Hubble telescope a space-based telescope, launched in 1990 and now in orbit around the Earth, that takes photographs of objects in space

light desk a desk or box with a lamp inside and white plastic over the top, used to look at transparencies

paparazzi photographers who seek photos of celebrities

photo shoot a session when a photographer is taking photographs

studio lighting electronic lights used to provide extra brightness inside a room

telephoto lens a camera lens that makes something that is far away appear closer in the photograph

transparencies slides that can be projected onto a screen, with normal colors (unlike photo negatives, which have reverse colors)

tripod a three-legged stand that supports a camera

INDEX